Dear Friends,

The Very Hungry Caterpillar was first published in 1969. Many times I have been asked where the idea for this book came from. One day, using a hole-puncher I playfully punched holes into a stack of paper. Looking at the holes I imagined a book worm could have done that, then the book worm became a green worm. Talking it over with my good editor Ann Beneduce the green worm became a caterpillar. Millions of children, parents and grandparents around the world have enjoyed my book, the story and the pictures. I must admit, I was surprised that my caterpillar became so popular and I am happy that the hopeful story of a little caterpillar turning into a beautiful butterfly has been enjoyed by so many. Thank you!

THE VERY HUNGRY CATERPILLAR

by Eric Carle

PHILOMEL BOOKS

ALSO BY ERIC CARLE

The Very Busy Spider
The Very Quiet Cricket
The Very Lonely Firefly
The Very Clumsy Click Beetle
1, 2, 3 to the Zoo
Animals Animals
Dragons Dragons
Draw Me a Star
Dream Snow
The Honeybee and the Robber
Little Cloud
Mister Seahorse
"Slowly, Slowly, Slowly," Said the Sloth
Today Is Monday

Copyright © 1969 and 1987 by Eric Carle.
Published by Philomel Books, a division of
Penguin Putnam Books for Young Readers,
345 Hudson Street, New York, NY 10014.
Penguin Young Readers Group,
First Published in 1969 by The World Publishing Company,
Cleveland and New York. All rights reserved.
No part of this book may be reproduced in any form
without written permission from the publisher, except for
brief passages included in a review. Manufactured in China.
Eric Carle's name and logotype are registered trademarks of Eric Carle.

Library of Congress Cataloging-in-Publication Data
Carle, Eric. The very hungry caterpillar.
Summary: Follows the progress of a very hungry
caterpillar as he eats his way through a varied and
very large quantity of food, until, full at last, he
forms a coccoon around himself and goes to sleep.
  [1. Caterpillars—Fiction.] I. Title.
PZ7.C2147Ve [E] 79-13202
ISBN 978-0-399-20853-9
71
Revised Printing

For my sister Christa

In the light of the moon
a little egg lay on a leaf.

One Sunday morning the warm sun came up and—pop!—out of the egg came a tiny and very hungry caterpillar.

He started to look for some food.

one lollipop, one piece of cherry pie, one sausage, one cupcake, and one slice of watermelon.

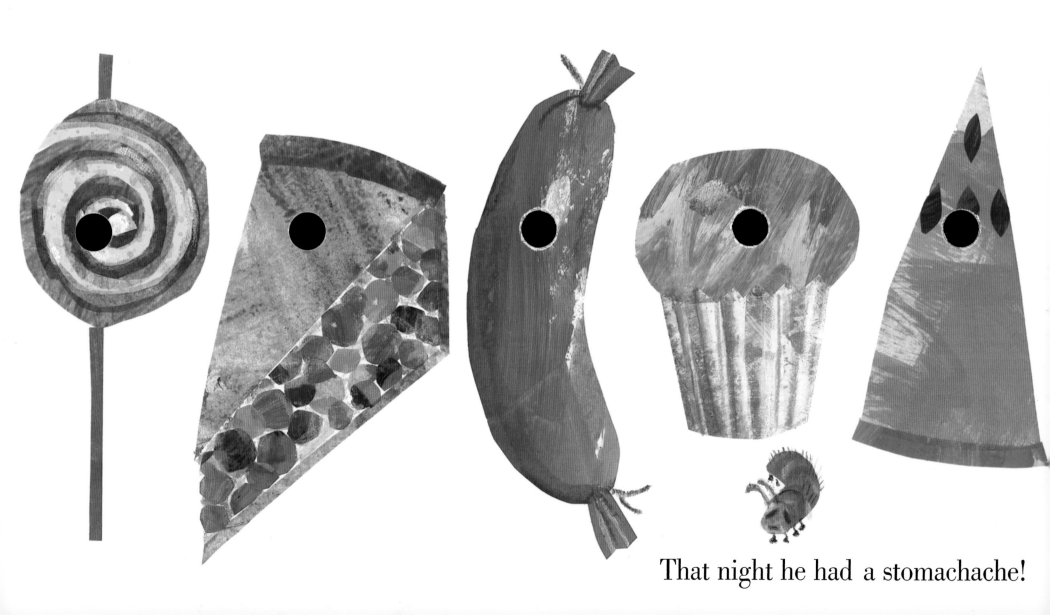

That night he had a stomachache!

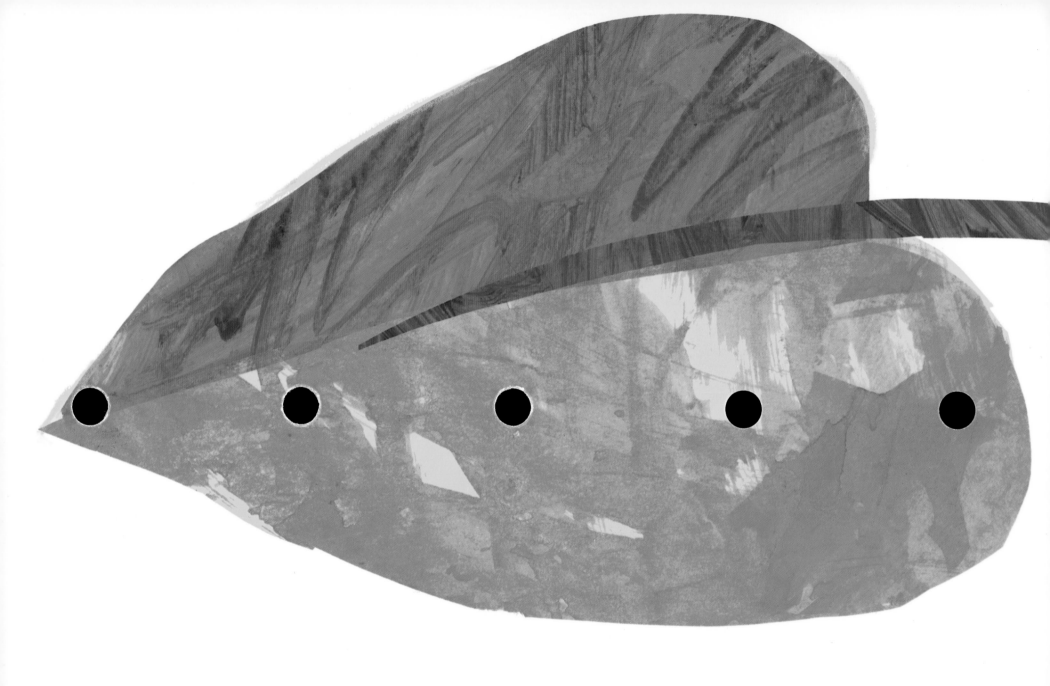

The next day was Sunday again.
The caterpillar ate through
one nice green leaf,
and after that he felt
much better.

Now he wasn't hungry any more—and he wasn't a little caterpillar any more.
He was a big, fat caterpillar.

He built a small house, called a cocoon, around himself. He stayed inside for more than two weeks. Then he nibbled a hole in the cocoon, pushed his way out and...

he was a beautiful butterfly!